One Bite Leads To Another

(A Once Bitten Novella)

By

Kelly Steel

Paradise Publication

Edited by: Nas Dean

Cover by: Jan Meredith

ISBN: 9789829810915

Title: One Bite Leads To Another

Copyright © 2015 by Kelly Steel

ONE BITE LEADS TO ANOTHER

Kelly Steel

After a spate of violence on his home island, Leonardo D'Silva returns home to find chaos on Lenuka Island. Who is responsible for this? And is the intriguing schoolteacher, Evelyn Hathaway connected to any of it? Face to face with Eve, Leo is taken back to the memory of his first love. Who is Eve? Is she a witch? And when Leo turns to his real vampire self after a night of passion with Eve, will she still accept him?

Evelyn Hathaway is intrigued by Leonardo D'Silva, the benefactor of her school, whom she's met for the very first time. Handsome, sophisticated and oh, so gentlemanly, she can't get him out of her mind. She's never met him before, yet she senses a strong connection, a feeling that they've met somewhere before. Who is this Leonardo D'Silva, with the hint of a demonic glint in his eye? Can it be possible...?

About the Author

Kelly Steel is a writer living in a slice of paradise. She has always read and with an overactive imagination started penning her own stories from a young age.

She lives in search of Happy Ever After for her characters and would love to connect with you, drop an email at ksteel924@gmail.com.

"Kelly Steel's 'One Bite Leads To Another' is a wonderfully compelling romance, with a sexy vampire hero, Leonardo D'Silva, and an enchanting heroine, Evelyn Hathaway.

Kelly Steel brings a wonderfully refreshing new twist to vampire romances with her multi-faceted characters, sensual storytelling style, and compelling plot. You'll love the surprises her heroine Evelyn brings to the story. This is a richly sensuous novella, the first in a series that will easily become addictive."

~ Lisa Weaver, Author~

"One Bite Leads to Another has lust, suspense, adventure, and compelling characters you probably don't want to meet in real life. The author's descriptions are lush and Eve and Leo's lovemaking scenes are intensely hot!

The novella length is perfect for my e-reader. I highly recommend this book to lovers of enduring love...and the paranormal."

"What a fun story! This is the first Vampire story I've read and I really enjoyed the folklore behind the characters and their motivations. A good read!"

From readers on Amazon

Dedication

To my husband Rajai and daughter Shariya for all your love and support. You may not know it but couldn't have happened without both of you!

And to Rani: I owe you. You are instrumental in turning all my dreams to reality!

Prologue

"Buy you a drink?" he asked the girl sitting next to him at a bar in downtown Sydney. He'd noticed her as soon as he entered. He planned to approach her, but she was openly scrutinizing him and now came to sit next to him. She was the only one not dressed in Gothic style in a group of girls who frequented this bar. She was a statuesque blonde and very beautiful. Like a predator, she eyed him hungrily.

"I say, we skip the drinks, honey. I can do without all these people," she said, her eyes challenging him to take up the invitation. She tilted her head to one side as she regarded him, which exposed the pale skin of her neck and the pulse that beat there.

As if, inviting him to sample. He hadn't even compelled her yet!

He was tempted to decline. There was no thrill without the chase. Nowadays some women were too easy. *Not like in the bygone days*, Leo thought to himself.

Then he thought better of it and took up the challenge. "I have a room upstairs." Centuries of life and later, time spent on the Wall Street stock markets, made it possible for him to amass quite a fortune. Jaded with an eternal existence of doing nothing, he lived his life on the edge and for challenges. It was very boring not to have the thrill of the chase. It didn't get the adrenalin rushing through him the way he liked.

"Let's go then." She led him to the elevator. On reaching his room, he closed the door behind him as he reached for her. He undressed her slowly, revealing each luscious curve one by one.

Their clothes shed; he took her hand and pulled her close to his muscular body, blood racing, and the demon inside sensing the promise of satisfaction held in her eyes.

"See," she said, "this is so much better without all those people."

"Or the clothes," he concurred. Taking her hand, he led her to the bed. Lying next to her, he pulled her closer.

He cupped her breasts in his palms. His vampire senses smelled her warm human blood and the beast needed the satisfaction of another kind. He drove the demon back. He wished to at least pleasure the woman, before he allowed his own release and indulged the vampire with a different kind of fulfillment. She smelled like spring flowers and felt like pure sin, the sultry combination warming his blood and setting the mood for the wonderful sensations to come.

He slid his hands down her firm waist, over long lean thighs, taking in all the smooth curves. He inserted his thigh between her legs and she rocked against it, slow and deliberate, as he licked and sucked her breasts. His tongue swept like liquid gold, covering her with the smooth sensation of satin drizzled over her skin. When he gripped her waist and thrust her against him, hot spasms of pleasure made her gasp.

"Mmmm," he moaned. "I take it you like that?" Trailing a finger down her belly, he stopped at the apex of her thighs. "How about more?"

She opened her mouth to answer, but before she could, he slipped a thumb between her thighs and stole the breath from her lungs.

She closed her eyes and groaned, her ability to do much else draining away with every smooth stroke. His fingers, legs, mouth, and chest all working together to bring sensation to every corner of her body. One moment he ground against her, the next he was on top, stroking his length along her core, teasing her towards the edge then changing motion right at the brink. He enjoyed keeping her at the height of arousal without granting her that heavenly release.

Leo couldn't think of anything sexier than watching a woman lose herself to orgasm. Nothing made him feel more masculine than being the one responsible for a woman shattering to pieces. Foil ripped and he sheathed himself.

Parting her legs he slipped inside, slow and easy, her smooth heat encasing him, snatching any more words from his throat and replacing them with a low, sultry groan. She fit him like a fine supple glove, her muscles contracting as he filled her in one long, hot stroke. Her soft moans drove him on, until he could hold no longer. He started thrusting into her repeatedly and she screamed from the force of his thrusts and the pleasure they wrought in her.

The pulse at her neck beat rapidly. Violently. Blood called him to fulfill another need. He could no longer keep the demon back.

Leo bent his head and placed his lips there. He licked her skin, finding it salty from the sweat of their lovemaking. Sweet beneath the sweat.

She shot him a look and he whispered against the side of her face, "You know what I want."

She was completely under his spell now. At her nod, he surged upward into her one last time, shuddering a climax that made her scream.

Finally freeing the demon as his eyes bled out and fangs erupted from his mouth. Fangs that he drove deep into the skin at her neck.

Her body tightened around him, held him closer as the vampire's kiss created a different kind of hunger within her.

Sucking, he savored her blood, singing with the passion from their lovemaking. Filled with youthful energy, as her blood charged every inch of his vampire body with renewed strength.

He could have kept on feeding, as others sometimes did. There was the choice to release the human after sating his hunger or let her die. Leo took only enough to sate the night's hunger.

His hands trembled when the energy zipped through his veins from his feeding, but somehow he managed to dress her and himself. A burst of vamp speed and he deposited her on the bench outside. Looking around he saw the park was deserted. Nobody saw him depositing her here.

As Leo gazed down at her, she seemed peacefully asleep. The bite marks on her neck had already healed. When she would awake, she would feel as if she merely had a bad hangover, and remember nothing of their encounter.

His mobile phone vibrated in his pocket, and with a last look at her, he moved off taking the phone out of his pocket.

Checking the caller ID, he saw it was Winston, his keeper in Sydney. "What's up, Winston?"

"Leo, I received a call from Peterson, he's trying to contact you."

"Okay, I'll be home shortly."

Sitting in the study of his bachelor pad, at Bondi Beach, one of Sydney's most exclusive locations, Leo answered the call. Peterson was his keeper from Lenuka, his home in Fiji.

"We have a problem, Leo, big trouble brewing up here on the island."

"What sort of trouble?"

"School children missing or turning up at home and school disoriented. Animals found slaughtered in the woods."

"And—"

"It's Zachary, with a couple of newborns causing havoc."

Zachary was a new vampire with limited powers but he couldn't control his feelings and turned violent very fast. Moreover, if he was with other newborns…utter chaos. Leo saw him in action late the previous year in Manhattan, when someone had aroused his wrath.

Zachary had to be stopped, if he was on the island.

"Okay, I'm taking the morning flight in, see you by early afternoon."

Winston regarded him, "You want me to come with you, Leo?"

"No, I'll check this out." Leo moved to his laptop and connected to the local airline's site to book his ticket.

In the morning, it took him three hours to reach his destination's main city. From there, another hour by a small domestic plane to the island, Lenuka.

Peterson was waiting for him, with more news. "The word is, Zachary's been thwarted and scorned by some girl from Lenuka, and he's turned up here for revenge."

"Any idea who that girl is?"

"He is shadowing a schoolteacher. I have no idea where they could have met as she's known never to have left the island."

"So now, who is this teacher to whom I have to play baby sitter?"

"Her name is Evelyn Hathaway."

A swoosh of air left Leo's lungs as he stared at Peterson.

"Evelyn…?" He asked, still trying to come to terms with what he heard.

"No, no, not her. She's her great-great-granddaughter. She's a teacher in the school. She lives here with her grandmother. Be prepared for a shock. She is the spitting image of her ancestor."

And shocked he had been when he'd first seen her.

Chapter One

"We haven't been properly introduced yet," Eve said, entering the staffroom and finding him alone. "I'm Evelyn Hathaway, but everyone calls me Eve."

"Leonardo D'Silva," he replied, extending his hand, "Leo to friends. Very pleased to meet you."

Shaking hands with him, Eve swore as a jolt of electricity shot up her arm. Puzzled, she tried to penetrate his mind, but was unable to do. Even more puzzling.

Oh, oh, so that's how it is. He's blocking me, so he's definitely hiding something!

Thanks to the legacy of her ancestors, Eve was blessed with special powers. She could read minds and even hypnotize people if she wished. Her grandmother, with whom she lived, was particularly powerful. Evelyn and her twin sister Eva, her grandmother's only living female descendants had limited powers as of now. This power had passed through the female line from generation to generation. Normally, on shaking hands with someone, Eve would've been able to read his thoughts. She could delve into most minds, but found that she was unable to do so now, in the case of this Leonardo D'Silva.

So what was he doing here in her small island school, if he was not what he seemed? He was new here. Eve was intrigued. Apparently in his early thirties, he was tall with rugged dark features and a strong self-assured presence which commanded attention. He had certainly drawn hers when she'd seen him earlier that day. She'd been unable to account for the uneasy feeling which swept over her when their eyes met. Her curiosity was immediately aroused. *Who is he? What does he really want?*

There were too many incidences happening on the island lately to ignore her misgivings. Students at the school were turning up for classes disoriented and lethargic. They were disinclined to study or pay attention in class. In the woods, at the back of her grandmother's house, she had seen animal carcasses strewn around with no apparent explanation of who was responsible. She had a premonition that something untoward was about to happen.

"Any relation to the D'Silva family?" She asked. The D'Silva family was one of the founding families of the island. They still maintained their original family home here, a huge mansion on the other side of the woods. It stayed empty, except for the white-haired old man, who lived there. Locals shunned the place as it was believed to be haunted. Moreover, there was even suspicion among the younger generation that the old man himself was the ghost.

"Guilty as charged, I am the prodigal son, returning to the family home." Regarding her with his dark, compelling gaze, he smiled. That smile transformed him into a rakishly charming and dangerously attractive man.

A sudden charm that was breathtaking. At least Eve felt breathless.

A fluttering deep in the pit of her stomach started as she looked at his six foot-two-inch frame. He had a loose-limbed graceful walk, and a chiseled look. Tilting her head to meet his gaze, she became aware of him with every nerve in her body. She was astonished to discover her body was humming. It was like tuning into his vibrations, a complete physical awareness. It was strange in spite of her misgivings. To complicate her mixed reactions to him, there was that charming smile of his which intrigued her.

This was a definite first for her, feeling attracted to someone she just met. Even stranger she'd been unable to read his thoughts. Breaking eye contact with him, Eve tried to compose herself. She picked up her papers and handbag and set out to walk home.

Darn it, he fell into step with her!

It was already dark outside as she'd stayed back for the school board meeting where their newly returned chairman of the board, Leonardo D'Silva, had presided. As he was normally an absentee chairperson, all the other members and teachers were encouraged to attend. Now standing outside, Eve could see the storm clouds' gathering. She knew the sign was ominous. There was a threatening chill in the air as they walked together, boding evil. Eve became aware of a menacing presence.

"You're going the wrong way," Eve said. "Isn't the D'Silva mansion on the other side of the woods?"

"I assumed you lived with old lady Hathaway, at the end of the road." Leo replied. "I'll just cut through the woods to the other side, after walking you home." With a hand at her elbow, he guided her over a rough patch on the path. "So who else stays with you?"

At his touch, she almost stumbled. She was quite unprepared for her body's volatile reaction to him.

"Oh, it's my grandmother and me since Eva's been away." She replied. "Not that she ever is home. Eva's my twin," she said. She was about to add more, then decided against it.

Normally Eve wouldn't have shared personal information with a stranger. But the strangest thing was apart from being attracted to Leo, she also felt an uncanny connection with him. Almost as if, she *should* know him. Considering the fact that she'd been unable to read his mind, this felt most peculiar to her.

However, now she knew he was from one of the oldest families on the island, at least she needn't be suspicious of him.

***

"Do you ever take holidays away from the island?" Leo asked her. Stunned by her appearance, he was tongue-tied. Apart from her hair, which was wavy and shorter, she looked exactly like his Evelyn…

However, she was not his Evelyn. Her style of dressing was totally different. Her whole personality was the opposite of her namesake's. She was an entirely different individual.

Leo tried to probe her mind, but was unable to do so as she blocked him. She seemed shielded as well. This was surprising. He hadn't expected her to be able to shield herself. Even if he couldn't delve into her mind, he could still sense Eve was a good person. He could actually feel positive vibrations shine through her personality.

He was drawn towards her like a magnet. She was very beautiful, almost exotic looking. She was petite with wavy hair. His hands itched to pull the pins holding her hair out and let it tumble down onto her shoulders. In all these years, he'd never seen another person as beautiful. He was fast drowning in her eyes and in her personality. The chemistry and awareness was so strong, he knew they would one day be lovers…

He had kept an eye on her the whole day without her being aware of him. Seeing Eve interact with her students and their parents, he knew she was kind and considerate towards all of them. She was also generous with her time, spreading hope and happiness to everybody. She was a very optimistic person and everybody seemed to like and respect her. He saw people walk away with smiles on their faces after meeting and talking with her.

He, too, was captivated by her. She had that effect on people.

"No, my grandmother is elderly. I don't like leaving her alone," she answered his question with a laugh, pulling him out of his reverie. "She'll kill me if she hears me say that. Then, there's my job, I can't leave wherever and whenever fancy takes me." Gazing at him, again that jolt of awareness passed, weakening her knees. The knot in her stomach twisted tighter.

Why is he asking all these questions? The thought ran through her mind. Turning around she started walking again. Even if he was the son of the founding pioneer family of the island, could she trust him? After all, what did anyone know of him? Just that he came from Australia every so often for the school's annual function.

But then, their school carried his family name and thrived from his donations. It was part of the D'Silva family's charitable trust, which was set up for the benefit of island people. As these thoughts went through her head, she put her misgivings aside. Chiding herself for her uncharitable thoughts regarding their benefactor, she turned towards him and smiled.

He was so breathtakingly handsome. Her heart fluttered like a butterfly. He had a traditional way about him, an *Olde Worlde* courteous way, which was very appealing. Eve's breath caught in her throat. In darkness, outlined in silhouette, he had the Greek God look, which absolutely overwhelmed her.

He left her with mingled reactions. One was an unconscious response to his innate sensuality, another was the sense that for whatever reason, he was about to turn her well-ordered life upside down.

Her face composed into a misty smile.

***

He already knew her. He was here on the island, especially to protect her. He'd come to the island following the phone call he'd received after that night in Sydney. But, he understood that this Evelyn was a different person altogether. She was more self-assured and stronger willed. She knew her place in the world.

But the pull was still there for him. Towards her.

And her life was in danger from Zachary and he had to find out why.

Chapter Two

If she'd never been away from the island, then where had she met Zachary?

Someone was disturbing the children of Lenuka. That someone was Zachary. As recently reported, there was quite a disturbance in the area, with schoolchildren turning up at home and school in a state of confusion. The only lead Leo had was Evelyn Hathaway. He was currently at a dead end. He'd come here to hunt Zachary down. To maintain the tranquility of his home island, he would do anything.

Leo walked with Eve with the intention of seeing her safely to the gate of the Hathaway house. He did not want Eve walking around in the dark. He could sense presence out in the woods.

A malevolent presence, which wished harm. His instinct warned him that a vampire was close.

He tried to hurry Eve along with a hand on her elbow. She stumbled and turned towards him with unease.

Did she also feel that jolting of senses he felt whenever he touched her? When he tried to delve in her mind, he could feel her blocking him out.

This was an added dilemma. He was very much fascinated with Evelyn Hathaway. He also noticed her desire for him in her eyes. Gazing deep into those green eyes, he felt the demon in him rising. He turned and took her in his arms.

All of a sudden, she seemed flustered.

"I…" She threw her head back, baring her neck.

Her pulse beat wildly under the skin. He could see the rapid twitch at her collarbone, could smell the blood now. The need to taste it, fed by the adrenaline ripping through him, almost overwhelmed him.

Leo froze. Her throat was long and pale.

He lowered his head.

She jerked again.

Leo's lip rose, and his fangs descended unseen in the dark. He had never wanted anything as much as he wanted to taste Eve's blood. He dipped his mouth towards her neck.

My God, what was happening? Eve found herself clinging to him. Her heart beat as if it might fly from her chest. Her instinct shrieked danger, but her body defied all the warning. Her knees bent, pushing her even closer, until she could feel his breath dance over her skin and her breasts flattened against him.

"What…what are you doing?" The words were no more than a whisper. She stared up at Leo, thinking it was strange that she'd met him for the first time today and he was making her body react in an even stranger manner.

His eyes were dark…dilated to the point she couldn't tell their real color. His black hair was, tousled, falling over his forehead and brushing one cheek. She wanted to push the strands back and run her hands in his hair.

He stared back at her and something clicked in his eyes. A circle of gray appeared, telling her their color. Then with a curse, he shoved her to the side.

Leo spun towards her. "Get inside the house," he ordered. With those words, little more than a growl, he raced towards the woods.

***

As he had been about to kiss Eve, Leo had felt Zachary's malevolent thoughts.

Which meant he was nearby. Watching them!

Reaching the edge of the woods, Leo didn't pause. He ran with a burst of vamp speed into the thick jungle.

As Leo entered the jungle, he focused on the job ahead and stopped thinking about Eve, just hoping she would go inside the house as he had ordered and resist thoughts of following him into the woods.

There was no moonlight to guide him and he paused to let his vamp sense guide him in the dark, under the canopy of trees. His fury knew no bounds. Leo sensed the newborns before he saw them. Newborns, former humans who, having just been converted by a vampire feeding from them, as yet immature in their way of handling their power and passion. Leo knew very well that newborns were almost uncontrollable. With a snarl, he charged towards one of them.

As he did so, he saw the short spike the newborn vampire whipped out from his pocket. Leo dematerialized and appeared behind the newborn.

The newborn vampire whirled. Leo lunged forward and twisted the newborns wrist, forcing him to drop the stake. The newborn fell with a thud to the ground, shoved hard by Leo against a tree trunk.

He dematerialized and appeared before the other newborns. There were three of them approaching him menacingly.

With the wooden handled dagger out in one hand and the wooden spikes in the other, he turned towards them.

The newborns were no match for Leo's speed or power. He felled them one by one. When all were down, he stopped and looked menacingly towards where he felt another vamp presence.

"I know you are here, Zachary, come out," he said ominously. Leo's age made his rank higher than Zachary's. Still he wondered if Zachary would heed his threat.

All of a sudden, Zachary materialized in front of him. His face thunderous, hands tightly clenched. Leo realized Zachary was barely in control of his aggressive self.

"You, of all people, also fell for her charm," Zachary said, his voice full of scorn. "I saw you being bowled over by her just now. But, let me tell you, she can't be touched. She is shielded somehow."

Leo spoke calmly, "Why are you here? This is my home and I don't want your type hanging around here..." He took a step towards Zachary, "No more newborns. I don't want the tranquility of this island to be disturbed. Leave this place in peace. Is that clear?"

"Oh, I had a lot of fun with the students. Not like you, depending on the frozen stuff from the soccer mums."

Leo ignored his taunt regarding the donated blood he drank from the blood bank while on the island. "Tell me why you are here?" He asked Zachary again.

"I came here to kill the b..."

Before he could complete the sentence, Leo jumped in with, "But why, what has she done? Tell me." He commanded quietly, with an authority in his voice that Zachary couldn't ignore.

All of a sudden, Zachary seemed depleted, all his violence spent. He put his head down.

Leo probed his mind. The images he saw of Zachary and Eve shocked him to the core.

"Is it true?" He asked Zachary quietly, unexpectedly sorry for the other vampire.

"Do not pity me." Zachary snarled. Back to his violent self. "I will bloody kill her. I don't need your pity." He suddenly dematerialized.

Leo was in a quandary. He knew what he'd seen, but he also knew Eve hadn't left the island. On the other hand, where was the proof that she hadn't? Which meant she'd lied to him.

He'd been so taken in by her looks that he hadn't seen beneath the surface. He'd let his attraction for her cloud his judgment.

Leo was thunderous with rage. At her, but more at himself. How could he let a mere human affect him so much? Hands clenching into fists, Leo became murderous at the very thought of her.

Realizing he was feeling jealous as well, of Zachary and the images he carried of Eve in his mind.

Then he reined in his feelings. He couldn't deny his instincts towards her, which said she was innocent of all that he was imagining about her. A piece of the puzzle was missing. Eve had said she'd never left the Island.

If nothing else, he had to trust in that and in his own gut instinct about her.

He was determined to reach to the crux of the matter fast. Instead of going towards his mansion, he turned towards Eve's home.

Knocking on her door, he felt a strange sense of foreboding. The door opened and her grandmother looked out at him, knowingly.

"You're not welcome in my house." She turned to close the door.

He tried to put his foot in through the door but he couldn't. Why?

The house seemed to be shrouded. No wonder Zachary hadn't reached his target before now.

He said quickly, before she could close the door. "Look Ms Hathaway, I need to speak with Eve…Evelyn for just a minute."

"Like I said, you're not welcome into my home. And don't try to come near my girl again."

"But you don't understand, there's someone—" Before he could complete the sentence, the door shut in his face with a bang. He stepped back. There was nothing he could do for the present. Unless, of course, Eve came out of the house. He couldn't materialize into the house. It was shrouded against vampires.

He could hear raised voices inside. Eve's angry voice mixed with her grandmother's.

As he stood there, undecided on what to do next, the door opened.

His breath caught in his throat. Eve stood on the threshold looking very beautiful.

"I thought you were in a hurry to go," she said, fuming.

She was angry with him. But why? Then he realized that she must have been upset because instead of kissing her, he had left her so abruptly at her gate earlier that evening...

"Look I'm sorry about what happened earlier. Will you take a walk with me?" he asked cajolingly, giving her a boyish smile and raking his hand through his tousled hair. "I'll explain."

Chapter Three

Eve stepped back into the house. Her grandmother looked at her ominously. However, she was also wringing her hands. Eve realized her Grandmother twisted her hands, when she was very nervous.

"Don't go, Eve, its dark and he's not who he seems. Besides, a storm is about to start."

Eve looked at her grandmother. "Don't worry Gran; I can take care of myself. Besides I know him from school." She put on her shoes and stepped outside the house. She knew whenever her grandmother was nervous; she started reliving her ancestor's turbulent life and journey here from England.

Through her grandmother, Eve knew the story about her ancestor after whom she was named who had been about to go into the flames, courtesy of peoples' ignorance in England at the time. But something or someone, had literally plucked her out of a dangerous situation and deposited her miles away, not to mention a century or two forward in time, on a ship. A ship, which was about to sail for Fiji, a new British colony. Mysteriously, a trunk packed with personal belongings, appeared in the berth she shared with others. After she made her life on the island, the only thing she regretted was that she never ever had the chance to seek out or thank her benefactor. Eve felt for the hardship and difficulties her ancestor had faced.

She didn't want anyone or anything to disrupt their peaceful life on the island either. However, for some reason, she couldn't ignore Leo's summons.

He was waiting near the gate. Feeling his magnetic pull she walked towards him.

***

Leo watched her and swallowed. His mouth was dry, his body ached.

She was built like the women of his youth, the time when womanly curves were celebrated, not starved away.

She'd taken a shower and her hair had fallen into fine waves on top of her shoulders. His fingers opened and closed. The locks would be soft to his touch. His hands itched to touch her. To run his fingers through her hair. To feel the texture against his mouth, chest and his body.

And her taste—his tongue moved over his fangs—would be sweet and addictive.

Then his mind flicked to the images he had seen of Zachary and her.

He should walk away. Let her deal with Zachary.

But he couldn't.

His foot heavy, he took a step forward. By then she reached him, smelling sweetly of frangipani. He couldn't focus on anything except her. Taking her hand, he led her through the hidden shortcut which only he knew. To the other side of the woods, straight to his house.

"Um, uh where are we?" she asked confused. With her hands held in his, she hadn't been aware of the surroundings.

"My house. We'll have privacy to talk here." He improvised. Opening the door, he ushered her inside. Telling himself his only motive was to keep her with him as long as possible so he could ask her a few pertinent questions. However, as he stepped in after her, he knew deep down that it was much more than that. He found himself lost in the intriguing green eyes, which held secrets he wished to unlock.

Eve sighed. Wondering how she would be able to keep her distance when the mere touch of his hand or even a simple glance from him sent waves of awareness racing through her.

She returned the gaze, which lured her like a magnet. She had feared that behind his smile, he might be able to see into her mind. To sense her thoughts. To hear the pounding of her heart.

Some emotion deep inside her responded to the way he looked at her. She forced herself to face a truth, which she'd been trying to ignore. The truth that Leo, with his sheer aura of innate masculinity had awakened feelings within her. Feelings which she'd never even known existed.

As they entered, the white-haired old man, who was lurking inside appeared before them. Eve saw him looking towards Leo enquiringly.

With a flick of his wrist, Leo dismissed him and the old man walked away to the back of the mansion.

Eve looked around. The mansion was palatial indeed. Then again, why not? After all, the D'Silvas' were a very wealthy family.

"Please sit down," he said, indicating a settee. "I'd like to ask you something."

Sitting down on the settee he had invited her to, she looked up at his face. She saw, with some surprise, that he was quite serious.

"Eve, please be truthful, this is a matter of life and death," Leo started, and Eve felt alarmed. "Have you ever left the island?"

"What's this, a quiz game? I told you before, I've never been off the island."

Leo could not dismiss the image of her and Zachary from his mind. "Are you sure?"

"Are you insane?" she asked, trying to quell her raising fury. "Don't you understand what I'm saying? And what did you mean when you said this is a matter of life and death?"

"We'll get to it later. Think carefully. Have you ever met a man named Zachary Vincent?"

"No and I don't have to think." She was quite angry now. "And if you are not telling me what this is all about, then I'm going home." She got up and walked to the door.

She was walking away.

No.

He wouldn't let her go…he *couldn't.*

He found himself across the room, his fingers molded to her firmness.

It was as if he'd electrocuted her. And vice versa. She stiffened; her flesh zapped a charge up his arms. With a long, pained groan, he dragged her back to him. She melted against him, all the missing parts of him fitting back.

He crossed his arms around her, melded her to his aching body, his hungry lips tracing a path up her neck until they closed over her ear lobe. She cried out with the first hot, hard pull, arched back into his arousal, her head rolling over his shoulder, giving him license to take, to own.

He scooped her up and clamped his mouth over her petal-soft lips. Leo groaned inside her delicious depths, drew more of her whimpers of surrender as he carried her to the nearest couch. He took her down on top of him, everything inside him roared for him to let go, take her now, brand her, and bind her. Whatever else there had been, her desire was real. He could feel it, scent it. And if her story checked out, he could forgive, forget. He could love her…

"No." She started pushing out of his hold, gasping.

He gazed at her, and she was lost in his eyes. Leo moved and took her in his arms again. She felt herself yielding and compliant.

His groin tightened.

Tension flowed from her body like water from a spring. He could feel it. She closed her eyes and tilted her head back as if relaxing. The thought that she was as comfortable in his embrace as he was embracing her flitted through his brain briefly. But again, Leo's attention focused on the column of skin which her movement had bared, her throat, pale and perfect.

The tiny steady throb of her pulse called to him. Leo had never fed from a human on the island.

That was why he spent all his time playing in Sydney and other metropolitan cities. Where he could feed from humans. Not here, not on his island.

Here on the small community of the island, they had a rule against feeding from humans. One of Leo's vampire friends was the director of the local hospital's blood bank. This friend had a very lucrative side business supplying his kind with blood. Every so often, he put a call out that the blood bank dried up. Then blood drives were held in public places. More blood donations flowed in and his kind were never out of supply. Moreover, the blood bank director's coffers filled up discreetly.

Leo brushed his lips over her collarbone and tried to remember who he was, the task he had to complete. Tried to think of newborns and vampires drunk with their own power, but all he could see, all he could feel at that moment was Eve. She was everything to him and for the first time in his centuries' old undead existence, he was powerless to resist.

Leo's lips brushed over Eve's throat. Some tiny bit of sanity told her this wasn't right. But as quickly as the thought flickered to life, she knocked it aside. Eve's hands moved to his chest, touching his smooth body through the crisp cotton of his shirt.

Leo crushed her trembling lips beneath his, swallowed her red-hot moan, feasting on her taste, her surrender.

This. This woman. This flesh. This connection. This was all that mattered. Time and place fell away at a touch, giving way to new realms…

Then he thought about a different Evelyn, in a different place. In England. His love. He had been on the verge of declaring his undying love to her, of asking her to be his wife, when a twist of fate had turned him to an eternally undead being, a vampire. He'd saved her and himself from the witch-burning flames in England and brought her here, but hadn't let her know it was him. He had settled near his Evelyn, forever her well-wisher and looking after her from far.

He had to stand by and see her marry someone else. He'd accepted her marriage and her husband. Then, her children.

As long as she remained his friend.

She did.

A very loyal friend. When she became a war widow, he was the one to console her. It was the same when she lost her son to the war as well. He was with her through all her tragedies.

She'd aged as most people do and died eventually, while he'd remained forever young. He cursed his fate for remaining the same while she was gone. He mourned her loss and his heart fragmented into tiny pieces. It was then he started going abroad. His heart never healed.

Until now.

When he came face to face with Eve.

Similar to her.

His Evelyn.

Chapter Four

Blood and a warm human body recalled him to present. He ground his hardness against her core through his pants. Her panties were damp with her desire, her nipples taut where he'd been touching them through the lace of her bra.

Making her straddle him by lifting her up, he looked into her face. Her eyes were half shut as if she was drowsy. He curled his hand around her neck and kissed her long and deep while with the other hand helping her grind down on his beyond painful erection. He groaned and tried to keep the demon within him curbed.

Nothing would satisfy him until he had her naked beneath him, his body buried into hers. His fangs sinking into her neck, drawing her delicious, hot blood.

"I want you, Eve. In my bed, naked beneath me and I won't stop until I have you."

He wanted to sink his fangs and his maleness deep inside her. Feed from her while possessing every luscious inch of her lovely body. Watch as her hair feathered over his pillow, her eyes closed with sheer pleasure as he brought her from one exhilarating peak to another.

The demon within him knew nothing of that. It knew only of the call of blood in her veins and the sex that roused it to violence.

Curbing his vampire self, Leo took her by the hand and led her into his bedroom. Closing the door, he leaned against it. Intent blazed in his eyes.

His vampire self had nothing to do with what was about to happen, since he refused to allow the demon to interfere tonight. He wanted Eve to experience all that a man and woman should when they cared for each other.

He couldn't deny that he'd cared for Evelyn back in the past and now, this Eve, as never before. His Evelyn, Eve's ancestor, he had put on a pedestal and had gone through all her happiness and tragedies with her. He had been her best and most loyal friend.

But now, he wanted Eve, this woman, this night, and to forget the woman in his arms had secrets.

"I can't promise you forever." He whispered, against her lips, thinking of his Evelyn. How she'd died after growing old.

"Neither can I."

Those words released his restraint, and he deepened the kiss. She accepted him, the thrust of his tongue and the promise of his arms. She reveled in the crush of his hard body, so big and muscular and pressed herself to him.

With a whirl, he carried her to the old-fashioned big four-poster bed. Setting her down on the side of the bed, he undressed her slowly.

When she was fully exposed, Leo cupped her breasts and caressed her nipples to peaks. She moaned and laid her hands on his shoulders, as her knees grew weak.

"You're so beautiful," he said, his eyes dark with desire. He put his mouth to one breast and tenderly sucked the tip. He caressed the tip of the other breast with his fingers.

Between her thighs, the pulse of her desire throbbed and thickened. She cradled his head with her hands and ran her fingers through his hair, urging him on with soft cries. His erection throbbed, needing attention.

Easing away from her, he kicked off his own pants and opened the buttons on his shirt, shedding it.

He met her gaze and held out his hand. "Come with me." He knelt on the bed, shifting until he was in the middle. Slowly he eased both of them down onto the sheet until they were lying with their bodies brushing each other.

Tenderly he reached up, cradled her face in his hands and kissed her. When Leo lifted one hand to her breast, Eve followed, tracing the edge of his nipple with her finger. She slipped her hand downward to caress him; he lowered his hand between her legs, parting her to find her center.

Eve sucked in a ragged breath as he eased one finger inside her. Raising her thigh, she slipped it over his, providing him greater access.

He felt her, wet and hot. And he wanted her—now.

She shifted to her back and guided him into her.

He slipped inside her tightness, overwhelmed by the sensation of her warm, willing body, accepting a man for the first time. By the tenderness of her kiss against his brow and the loving caress of her hand across his face before she sank down onto the mattress and met his gaze.

He saw it then. The love he never expected to see in his immortal life. The promise of so much more than just the physical release their bodies craved. The emotion was so strong, it nearly undid him and he closed his eyes, focusing on the union of their bodies.

He moved tentatively at first, acclimatizing himself to the feel of her beneath him, the tightness around him, slick with the passion he had earlier aroused.

She whispered his name, an entreaty to take her further, and he pushed, increasing the strength of his thrusts until all that could be heard was the sound of their breathing in the quiet night. Her knees came up around him, and her hands held tight to his shoulders.

He needed more. He needed to taste her, so he bent his head and sucked one breast, making her moan.

She held his head to her and arched her back, giving him greater access.

He felt it then, the beginning tremors of her climax rising from deep within her body. He gave himself over to the sensations of loving her.

The sensation and smell of her arousal and of the blood surging through her body.

The beast protested then, clamoring to be set free, but Leo battled the vampire back as he had earlier and thrust into her repeatedly until her body climaxed beneath his and she cried out his name.

Now his body jerked with pleasure and it began then, pooling at his center and moving outward.

Heat. Strong. Demanding heat. Uncontrollable desire.

He bent his head, the vampire beginning to assert control as the strength of its passion drove back the human, who had not experienced such joy in centuries. As Leo buried his head in the crook between her neck and shoulder, her pulse beat madly against the vamp-sensitized skin of his lips.

The blood called to him and Leo lost it.

The demon erupted even as he savored the release of his body.

Leo reared away from her, trying to rein in the vampire, who wanted nothing more than to sink his long, lethal fangs into her neck, but it was too late.

She had seen his true face and recoiled, scrambling away from him as he knelt before her on the bed.

"Please don't go, forgive me." He pleaded, as he held out his hands before him entreatingly.

Her hands crossed against her chest to hide her nakedness... "What are you?" she asked.

"I'm a vampire."

Eve shook her head in disbelief. "A vampire? A blood sucking vampire?"

The proof was there, in the strange blue-green gleam of his eyes and the white fangs that reached to the middle of his chin.

Despite that, she shook her head and closed her eyes, as if the image might somehow change. However, when she opened them, the demon remained though he was fully clothed. In Leo's clothing. His own clothes, she reminded herself. The creature before her was still Leo.

No wonder she had been unable to probe his mind and read his thoughts.

She swung her legs over the side of the bed, reached for her clothing and dressed quickly.

Leo wanted to charge after her as she left. Then he heard it. Muffled sobs.

His heart lurched. He didn't know what to do. He morphed back to his human self. Maybe she needed space.

But what happens when she goes outside? Into the dark...

To hell with space! Leo leaped out of the bed.

A low scream sent his blood racing. Leo, with a burst of vamp speed, was downstairs. As he headed for the front gates, he hoped he wasn't too late to help Eve.

Chapter Five

As she stepped out of the door, something grabbed her in a blur of movement.

In a daze of confusion, she couldn't get her bearings and then she realized she was in the middle of the woods. Someone had transported her there in a flash. Eve felt herself swallowed up in the labyrinth of the jungle.

She struggled to focus, when the hand around her throat squeezed harder and her vision faded as she lost consciousness.

***

Coming out of his gate, Leo stood still trying to ascertain which direction Eve had taken. He realized Eve had been emotionally upset and Zachary had taken advantage.

Seeing someone come towards him he froze. It was Eve, but there was something different about her. She was dressed differently. She even walked in a different way.

He stared at her as she came nearer. Tried to probe her mind but she blocked her thoughts. He looked and then looked again. She wore a ring in her pierced belly, where her midriff was bare, showed through her tank top and mini skirt.

How can this be possible?

"Eve—" Leo murmured.

"Have you seen Eve? I've looking everywhere for her. Grandmother said she'd been gone a while," the girl said, sounding apprehensive.

Then Leo realized something. "You must be Eva," he said.

"Yes, I'm Eva Hathaway. Evelyn, or Eve as we call her, is my twin."

Realization hit Leo hard. It all made sense now. His Eve hadn't been lying. It was Eva whom he'd seen in Zachary's images.

Zachary!

A knot twisted in Leo's gut. Zachary had Eve. He knew it.

"I think I know where Eve might be. Come with me." He started running towards the middle of the jungle, from where he had begun to sense the presence of other people. With Eva following, he was unable to use vamp speed. Therefore, he went as fast as he could and when he came upon a clearing, he stood stock-still.

Big, ghostly hands were clamped around Eve's throat, squeezing so hard that the knuckles were white as bone. It was Zachary. He had Eve. He was about to sink his fangs into the side of her neck.

Leo looked towards Eva. She was also standing immobile as she surveyed the scene before her.

Then she moved forward.

She seemed to be concentrating on Zachary. She was staring straight at him and not at Eve, as he expected. Then Leo heard her chanting. Leo understood. About Eve. About Eva. About their lives. About, how Eve had managed to block his mind probes. They were both endowed with the same sort of psychic power.

It was then that Zachary became very still. Then he turned and saw Eva with Leo, and he dropped Eve to the ground.

"Leave her alone. It's not her you want, it's me." Eva cried out.

Leo ran to Eve, and cradled her tenderly in his arms. She was nearly unconscious but her pulse was beating. He heaved a sigh of relief when she opened her eyes and looked at him.

"Leo, um what's happened?" She asked, looking towards Zachary. Then she saw him holding Eva. Zachary was looking into Eva's eyes and she gazed back at him.

Eve looked towards Leo and saw he was also looking towards them. Then Eve probed into Zachary and Eva's mind and a slew of images flew towards her. As her twin, Eva was unable to block Eve.

Chapter Six

A short time previously, Shanghai, China.

Eva Hathaway was on the stage. When she performed, everyone's eyes were on her movements on the stage. She was a dancer with an international dancing troupe and tonight they were performing at Shanghai's Expo Pavilion. It was said of her that she bewitched her audience while she performed…

While going through her dance movements, Eva skimmed the crowd and her eyes settled on a tall man with fascinating blue green eyes. She began to perform for him exclusively. Her body gyrated seductively and her eyes bewitched him. She normally chose some unsuspecting man from the audience to have fun with, later in the night. The sexual thrill, of performing as an exotic dancer in front of such a big audience required sensual outlet for her. The sexual throb of such dancing was very thrilling and excitement was as electricity in the audience.

Watching Eva on stage, Zachary felt the heat of her movements. He sucked in a shaky breath, feeling the pull of her even across the distance of the pavilion. Feeling himself harden and rise from the spillover of her ardor, he tried to keep control. She shifted her hips back and forth, and he had to grip the edge of his seat as that movement transferred itself to him and his erection strained painfully against the tight fabric of his jeans. He felt the demon rise within him for a taste of what she promised with her actions. He curbed the demon, promising fulfillment later.

All the while, Eva kept her gaze locked with his, clearly conscious of her effect on him. Increasing her caresses and movements until he was nearly undone, she finally broke her bewitching glance from him. Ending the program, the troupe took their bows and left the stage.

After some time, Eva came towards him with purposeful strides.

Without a single word said, they moved off in tandem towards a dark corner of a side room in the pavilion. With urgent hands, Zachary removed her clothing and had the first rewarding sight of her nakedness. Her breasts were full. Her nipples hard with her passion. The shade of golden honey, a surprise given her dark coloring. The mere perfection of it nearly did him in right there and he had to hold for a moment, staring into those beautiful green eyes while he waited for his anxious body to calm. And the demon to stay curbed. As he stared in her eyes, willing to comply, he was shocked to find that she was blocking him.

As Eva felt his powers come against her, some shred of self-preservation pushed her passion aside and she blocked his compulsion. When she used her power on him and became aware of his thoughts about her, she pulled her invisible shroud around her and melted into the darkness.

Seething when his hands felt empty air where Eva had been seconds earlier, Zachary punched a hole in the wall. The beast demanding satisfaction was uncontrollable. Trashing the room, he flew from that place with vamp speed.

The next night Zachary came again, but the dance troupe was minus one dancer. He turned on his charm and befriended the members of the troupe. Then he enquired about the missing dancer. "I seem to recall a certain dancer here yesterday, but she's nowhere to be seen tonight. Where can I contact her?"

"Oh the Hathaway girl? She had an emergency at home and left."

With a compelling gaze, Zachary asked where Eva's home was. "Lenuka." came the reply.

So Lenuka it is and here I come.

That was how Zachary had ended up in Lenuka, looking for Eva. In his rage, when he'd seen Eve, Eva's twin, he'd focused on her.

Eve again looked towards Leo and saw he had probed their minds and had seen the truth as well.

Then she understood why Leo had queried her earlier about her movements. So he knew about Zachary all along. In addition, he kept quiet about it.

Then he seduced her. And…and he was a blood-sucking vampire!

Chapter Seven

Leo moved towards Zachary and Eva. He wanted to keep Zachary in check, just in case he turned violent towards Eva.

He shouldn't have worried. Zachary seemed enthralled by Eva. Leo watched as those two kept gazing at each other. Zachary was still in vampire mode. With his eyes bled out and white fangs hanging down to his chin. Leo took a moment to reflect. Eva didn't seem in the least repulsed or frightened by the vampire which Zachary undoubtedly was.

As he watched, Zachary slowly morphed back to his human self.

Eva held out a hand to Zachary. "I'm Eva Hathaway."

Zachary gave a very chivalrous bow over her hand and shyly taking her hand, he kissed her knuckles. "My name is Zachary Vincent. And I'm delighted to make your acquaintance."

All of a sudden, Zachary dematerialized and disappeared from there.

Then Eva turned towards her twin. Her expression still bemused.

"Eve, are you alright?" she asked.

"What was all that about? And Eva, where did you come from? You haven't been home in ages." Eve queried her sister.

Eva turned to look once again, where Zachary had been standing. "Long story. Tell you another time." Then she turned her attention towards Leo. "You must be Leonardo—"

"Sorry I didn't introduce myself earlier. As you can see I was in a hurry." Leo gave a wry smile, looking at Eve. "I'm Leonardo D'Silva." He gave her an exaggerated bow, which made Eva laugh.

"Okay, we'd better be on our way, Grandmother will be worried." Eve said shortly, refusing to look at Leo. Her thoughts were in turmoil. It would take her a while to work out everything that had taken place. Her mind seemed blank. *Maybe I'm still just in shock by the near death experience.*

The sisters turned in the direction of their house and Leo fell into step with them. All the while they walked, Eve was aware of Leo's compelling gaze upon her. She didn't turn her head to look at him.

At their gate, Eva said goodnight to Leo and Eve also murmured something in response to Leo's goodnight. She still refused to meet his eyes. She couldn't dispel the image of Leo from her mind.

Leo as the vampire.

***

The next day, while catching up, Eve was discussing the events of the previous night with Eva. When they had reached home, their grandmother kept fussing around them. They'd made up a story for her about being out late, caught in the stormy weather, and blocked their thoughts from her probes. She seemed satisfied with their explanation and happy to have Eva home after a long time, so she didn't query too much. After all, she was old now and her power was no longer at its peak, as it had once been.

"Were you not frightened by Zachary the vampire?" Eve asked her sister.

"He is the most exciting man I've ever met," Eva replied, "Especially when he was in the vampire mode. And as you know, I've met many men, all over the world."

"Then why did you run away from him in Shanghai?"

"I got frightened by the intensity of his feelings and probably overwhelmed by mine as well. I wanted to run and hide myself away and I did. However, I couldn't do this forever. So, I decided to come home and talk everything over with you. Then who do I find when I get here? Him! Of all people!"

"I can't understand why you don't feel repulsed by him."

"Well, I didn't. I happen to find him most exciting and talk about sexy! Did you see the way he kissed my hand? Oooh, he's intriguing!" she said, her voice bubbling with excitement.

Eve couldn't believe her ears. Then her mind turned to Leo. She knew she was just as attracted to him. That nice, charming man he'd been before he made love to her—before he'd turned into that— thing!

How could she still feel any attraction or love for him now? After she'd seen the demon which was his true self?

A picture flashed into her mind of his dejected face before she'd stormed out of his house the night before. To her surprise, she felt a sharp pang of regret.

Hey? She felt sorry for him?

She realized then that she had deeper feelings for him. It must be so lonely and difficult to have eternal existence and no one to love.

Feeling extremely sad and depressed, she left Eva for a while and went up into the attic, alone. She always went to the attic when she felt sad or unhappy for some reason. She felt closer to her great grandmother there. The place was full of chests and trunks containing the belongings of all her many relatives and ancestors who had long since passed away. Sometimes, she would open a chest and rifle through the old-fashioned dresses. Afterwards she would feel calm as if connecting with her ancestors had blessed her.

Today, however, she sat on the rocking chair and just rocked herself. Her mind was in turmoil.

She was nearly on the verge of sleep when she noticed an old leather trunk underneath all other trunks and chests. Somehow, she felt she had never seen this one before now.

Getting up, she walked over to it. After removing all other trunks stacked on top of it, she pulled it out. Sitting back on her haunches, she opened it. Looking through the old dresses, she saw these outfits were not only old-fashioned but maybe not from here at all. These dresses were from Victorian England. Then she understood. She was opening her namesake's trunk. Could this be the trunk that had mysteriously appeared in the ship when the first Evelyn had set sail for Fiji?

Her fingers touched something hard. Pulling it out she saw it was a journal. An old leather covered journal whose pages were yellowed and falling with age.

Her great-great-grandmother's journal?

Opening it, she saw it was written in the ornate handwriting of another age. Taking the journal, Eve settled herself into the rocking chair. She opened it in the middle just to glance through it.

Stopping to stare when she saw Leo's name. His name was given as Leonard Shelton. According to what had been written by the first Evelyn Hathaway, he was adopted as a son by the wealthy D'Silvas' in Lenuka after befriending that family, who had no son and heir. Heart thumping hard as she started to read from the first page.

While tears streamed down her face, she read to the end of the journal. Looking outside she saw it had turned dark. Picking up a light jacket in her room, she put the journal inside her jacket, zipping it up and got ready to go and see Leo.

What if Leo didn't want to see her, after the way she'd behaved? But it was imperative they meet, especially now. She had to talk to him. For the sake of the first Evelyn Hathaway.

More for herself. Because she realized, with a sudden jolt, that she loved him with all her being. She didn't want to lose him.

If she wanted to have her love, she had to act fast. Then the unbidden image came into her mind. Leo. As a vampire.

Chapter Eight

Nobody was around when she reached Leo's house.

She knocked on the door. A moment later the door flew open and he stood before her. The practiced smile on his face turned to a scowl as he realized who the caller was.

"What do you want?" he asked, his voice a low rumble. As she met his gaze, the grey of his eyes slowly bled out to the scary blue-green neon of the demon and a menacing hint of fang dropped from his top lip.

"You can't scare me away, Leo."

She hoped she sounded calm and in control. After reading the journal, she now knew that he would never hurt her.

Leo examined her. He let his vampire senses take in everything about her.

"I thought you didn't want to see me again." His tone was cold, almost cruel, because anything else would move them towards perilous ground.

He was unapproachable in this mood.

Wincing as if struck Eve blanched. Color drained from her face. Despite that, she gathered herself, pulling her shoulders back beneath her chocolate brown jacket. She walked towards him and cradled his jaw tenderly.

He flinched, her touch cold on his skin.

She rose on tiptoe and whispered against his lips, "I'm sorry for my behavior towards you, but I'm not sorry about what happened between us."

In a space of a heartbeat, she'd kissed him lightly, then fled.

Leo stood rooted, his hands balled into fists, his gut twisted into a knot. He took a faltering step, about to follow her, and then remembered the lunacy of caring for a human.

Holding fast, his muscles trembling from the strain, he reached out with his vamp senses and picked up her essence as she hurried away.

Closing his eyes, he focused on it, memorized it, until it faded.

As it would fade when she died, as his Evelyn had died.

His best friend Evelyn. His love. He had loved her, wanted to make her his own.

But not as he loved Eve now. The thought came unbidden to him. It hit him like a punch in his stomach. Yes, he loved Eve. He admitted to himself. Trying to save her life from Zachary, he had fallen for her.

But there was nothing to be done now. There was no hope for them. There would be no happy ever after for them. He would always remain the same, while she would wither away and die of old age.

Once again, he had to hold back and leave her free to marry and be happy with someone else. Once again, his heart would fragment into tiny pieces.

Now he'd found her, made love to her, he'd find it difficult to step back. But he had to, for her sake.

Chapter Nine

"Are you going somewhere?" Eve asked nervously. She was determined to talk to him. She came again to see him the next morning. A morning that had turned out bright and sunny.

Hoping to find him in a better frame of mind, instead she found him packed up and ready to go.

She was sitting in his lounge, while he paced around like a caged up panther. His pacing around made her even more nervous.

"I'm off to Sydney." Leo answered curtly. He was hurt and bewildered by her earlier behavior. Going away from the island seemed a sensible solution.

"I'm sorry for not understanding you better." She told him. "This opened my eyes." She showed him the journal.

"What is it?" He sounded harassed, "I'm leaving shortly. I don't have time to discuss anything with you. Don't play any more games with me."

"No games. It's my great-great-grandmother, Evelyn's journal."

All of a sudden, Leo went still and alert. "Evelyn's journal?"

"Yes, her journal. That's the place where you write your private thoughts and feelings." She couldn't resist teasing him.

"I know what journals are!"

Eve turned sober. "It seems we have a lot to learn from her. Leo, she loved you all her life."

"What? She never said anything. She never told me. We were the best of friends. Family friends."

"Yes, she waited for you to tell her. That you were a vampire. She encouraged your confidences, but you never confided in her about your true self."

"She knew?"

"Yes, she suspected. She also suspected you were the person who saved her from the witch burning." Feeling sorry for Leo and her distant grandmother, Eve said. "When you didn't say anything, she married an Englishman she met on the island. She was content in her marriage and family. She regarded you as a good friend and was very pleased you were part of her family."

"Yes, she was very happy with her husband and children. I didn't want to burden her with my problem at the time." Leo remembered sadly. "So I tried to be her friend, but it broke my heart when she died."

"I don't think, I can be that brave, loving you but moving on with my life." Eve remarked.

"She knew—?"

"It seems she could read your mind when you were not actively blocking. She tried to make it easier for you, but you were very circumspect."

"Yes, I loved her and wanted to marry her. I planned on asking her, the same night I went to a tavern." He recounted. "I met a friend and we had few drinks. Coming home, I saw a beautiful woman in front of me. After compelling me, she then seduced me before feeding from me. She left me for dead."

He was laying there half-dead, when he saw another woman before him. He thought he had died and was in heaven. However, this kind woman helped him to shelter. She let him feed from her wrist to make him stronger. She saved his life that night and later became his lifelong friend. In the process, he turned to being a vampire.

Then he decided he couldn't marry Evelyn. He couldn't burden her with his demon self now. His sweet Evelyn. When he saw her taken away, he couldn't *not* do something to help her. He saved her and took her to the ship. He'd had to use super vamp speed to do that and in the process, the ship they landed on was in a few hundred years in the future. She was too distraught at the time. He went back and found a packed trunk, which he brought back for her. Then they came to this island and remained friends until she died. He recounted this story to Eve now.

"I watched her get old and die. I couldn't stop her. I didn't want the same thing happening to us."

"What are you saying? You love me?"

"Yes, I love you. But I can't watch you get old and die, like Evelyn did." He turned a sad face towards her. "After Evelyn, I survived, because I had not touched her. My love for her was wholesome. I never lusted after her. And I had a unique connection, a special friendship with her."

"But with me—?"

"I love you with everything in me. I wouldn't be able to see you old and withered, while I remained the same."

"What if I tell you, I'm prepared to live with you for all eternity?"

"No! I'll not turn you," he shouted.

"You don't have to turn me. My ancestor found something in her books, which were in the trunk you brought her. After finding out you were a vampire, she consulted her books." She told him jubilantly. "We, meaning the female line of my family, already have certain genes. This is why vampires attract us. Remember her, Eva and now me."

"What do you mean?" Leo couldn't think clearly now. He was in too much turmoil.

"I mean we can have our happy ever after!"

"How—?"

"We can have eternal life if we mate with a vampire and let him feed from us. But we don't turn into vampires!"

Leo was flabbergasted by all he heard.

How was this possible?

And why had Evelyn never told him?

In a way he was glad, because while he remained her lifelong friend, loved and respected her, what he felt for Eve, now, was very different. Very passionate.

"I'm glad you were there for my ancestor, Leo. You saved her and befriended her. She was happy in her marriage but as an added bonus you were there for her." Eve reassured him. "Her very best and loyal friend for all her life. It's all in her journal."

Leo looked at Eve. Her good character shone through. *Oh, how he loved her!*

Leo moved forward and took her in his arms. He kissed her.

Eve tenderly cradled his face with her hands and rained kiss after kiss against his face.

"In your arms, I feel as if I'm in an island of safety in a sea of perils." She told him.

Leo knew then that Eve was right. They had their happy ever after, after all.

Chapter Ten

"No, I can't allow you to marry him." Eve's Gran said the next morning. "He's not a mortal being…"

"I know what he is!" Eve replied.

"Still you want to marry him?" Gran was definitely not happy about it. "What about future generations?"

"What about future generations?"

"Well, he's undead and you can't give birth to his child. What if he harms you in his passion?"

"Leo would never harm me." Confident of that at least, she replied.

"Well, I'm not willing to go to my grave without seeing my powers passed onto a future generation."

Eve felt stumped. How could she convince her grandmother now? Looking at her grandmother, Eve saw she was adamant. Leo and she confessed their love for each other and she thought life would be smooth sailing now. She hadn't envisioned her grandmother's disapproval.

"There's Eva. She'll get married and give you your future dynasty!"

"Oh no...no. Don't even think about it. I'm not marrying ever," Eva replied. "And just for your grandchildren, no way." Eva said now, she had been quiet so far but when Eve turned to her, she defied.

Leo had wanted to come with her when she told her grandmother but she hadn't thought there would be any opposition to their plans. She tried again.

"But, Gran, we love each other."

"Yes, I know, but for the sake of future descendants and for our special power to move down the line, I forbid you to even think about marrying him."

Eve looked toward her twin. "How can I ignore my feelings for him?" she asked her sister. Eva shrugged her shoulders.

Swallowing back a sob, her head down and trying to control herself from breaking down, she went up to her room.

She ignored the knock on the door. Eva opened the door and tentatively stepped in.

"Thanks for the support down there!" Eve berated her.

"Look, I can't openly oppose Gran, you know that," she replied. "But I came to you with a solution."

"What solution?" Eve asked, intrigued despite herself.

"Oh, you'll like my simple solution, I tell you." Eva said airily.

"Ok, what is it?"

"Why don't you...um..." she started floundering. "You know..." she began again.

"No, I don't know," Eve told her. "What do you want to say?"

"Well, you can always go out with Leo and…" Eva squirmed again.

Eve paused. What was her twin saying? Her sister was the very modern, ultra-woman. She used men and discarded them without a single thought, so why was she finding it difficult to voice whatever she wanted to say?

"And…?"

"And enjoy yourself without getting married!" Eva finished quickly. "Gran wouldn't know and maybe you'll find you're not so suited to each other as you think you are, and maybe you won't want to marry the guy after all." Breathless and flustered after this very long speech, Eva took a long breath.

"Oh Eva, you don't understand, do you?" Eve said softly. "He's my soul mate. I wouldn't be able to live without him."

"I'm not saying for you to live without him," she replied. "But maybe things would change."

"No, our feelings for each other will never change." Eve replied adamant. "But why doesn't Gran understand?"

"Give her time. Maybe she'll come around."

"I don't think she will. She's after the future generations. What about me, here, now?"

Eve was desperate to escape the cottage after dinner. When darkness descended, she stole out and went towards the woods. She needed to see Leo and reassure herself that all was right between them.

In the woods, shadows from the tall trees fell across the path like ghostly figures as she walked deeper into the forest. The chirping of the birds stopped, the sound was ominous.

She whirled around when she felt a presence at her back. And saw Zachary Vincent standing there. Very handsome and dashing and not a bit scary like the other night.

"Eve, I presume?" he asked.

Heart thumping, Eve held out her hand, "Eve Hathaway, Eva's twin," she replied. Her fingers felt clammy with sweat and the hairs at her nape were prickling but she didn't want to show him she was scared.

Zachary bent low over her hand and kissed her fingers. Very old-fashioned and gallant.

"I beg you to forgive me and my misunderstanding the other night, please?"

"Oh, there's nothing to forgive. I understand, you mistook me for my sister."

"I was angry with her and when I came here and saw you…"

"It's okay. Since childhood I've been in trouble for something she did," Ava replied lightly.

Coming out from the woods, she turned to find Zachary had vanished. With a smile, she went to the door of Leo's mansion.

"Come in. You seem very pleased." Leo opened the door to her and eagerly took her in his arms.

"Guess whom I just met?" Returning his kisses, she asked.

"Ummm…nice!" Leo murmured, kissing her again. "Whom did you meet?"

"Zachary."

Leo held her away to look at her, "Did he…?"

"No…no," she replied, pleased to see him worried about her. "He apologized profusely and said he regretted causing me any harm."

Bemused, Leo hugged her again and started kissing her. "You okay?"

Mesmerized by his gaze, she could only nod.

"Good," he murmured against her lips. "Let's see if we can create some magic of our own."

As much as Leo needed Eve right now, he was afraid to push her too hard. Sometimes she looked too fragile.

But he knew about the sensual creature that lurked inside Eve Hathaway. And knowing that was making him crazy.

He'd seen it. Seen for himself on that insane night before he'd lost control and let the demon inside him emerge. He knew she had more power and strength of spirit than she could possibly know. Her own potent force shined right through the darkness.

Leo felt compelled to bring that out in her again. Was he selfish? Because in truth her strength turned him on almost more than he could handle.

No. He just had to see it again and again. Had to have that power under him, surrounding him. He craved it, with body and soul.

The silken lips he'd been fantasizing about were only a whisper away. Right here, right now. Closing the gap between them he was feeling more aroused than he could ever remember.

Their kiss began as a reverent touch of lips. But when she opened her mouth, he heard a moan coming from deep inside her body, Leo lost whatever was left of his control.

He deepened the kiss, using his tongue as a token, a symbol of his need to sweep aside her fears. He tasted and drank her very essence.

And then he slipped beyond all redemption. He managed to keep his control over the beast in him, but lost himself in the power of the sweetness and harmony he found in her embrace.

Leo felt her trembling and growing weak-kneed. He wrapped his arm around her waist protectively; and fitted her body to his own. The match was perfect, as he'd remembered. She was his other half. Just as if she'd been created specifically to be that one spark he'd felt had been missing from his life.

"Touch me," she urged in a hoarse whisper. "Please Leo. I want…"

Smiling, he placed his lips in the hollow between her shoulder and her neck, and at that contact, she arched and groaned. The pulse beating there and the blood pounding called to him. Crazed by the taste of warm skin and by the idea of what he could do to her by using his lips and teeth.

Leo had never experienced anything as intense as he had with Eve and now he craved for more. He felt an overpowering urge to lose himself in her lush body again. Be surrounded by her sweetness. He picked her up, carrying her upstairs to his bedroom. Then he let her slip down to her feet by the bed.

Slowly he lifted her tee over her head. Then he cupped her breasts in his hands and kissed the tips. He heard her moan when he ran his tongue across her throat and captured her lips.

When he kissed her again, she knew she was ready. Her body was on fire for him. It sizzled and sparked for him. Her clothes felt heavy on her body. She wanted them off and wanted to burn herself in his embrace. Drowning in his eyes, Eve drew a sustained breath that helped control the shaking of her knees. His hand went to the drawstring of her track pants. He pulled it down and went down on his knees in front of her. Fire streaked through her. She could hardly breathe in anticipation for what would be next.

"You're so beautiful," he murmured. His mouth hovered over her most sensitive spot. Then he kissed her there. His tongue slid over her, nibbling, sucking and flicking. Over and over again. She anchored her hands on his head. Her fingers grasping his hair while she thrust her hips forward. With one last sweep of his tongue she came apart. Her breath was sucked from her body and she felt helpless against the onslaught of her feelings. She almost went down to her knees. But Leo's hands held her up. It was too much. It was primal and raw and as much as she wanted to stop, she also wanted to go on and reach the next peak. She wanted him inside her now. Wanted to feel his hard but silky length sliding in her body.

Laying her down, Leo leant in and kissed her. Firm lips tightly leashed with control yet full of dark emotions as he took her mouth and showed her all his pent up desire.

For a moment sanity resurfaced and she pulled back reluctantly. "Can you…?" she asked tentatively. "…um…hold back the…uh…?"

His eyes burned into hers and promised restraint for the demon. "At this moment, I need you held against my heart."

That was all she wanted to do. Feel every glorious inch of him against her; be crushed by his power and reborn with his possession. She had to stop fighting her logical thinking and go with her emotions once again. She would think rationally later. She would let the sheer magnetism of this man draw her. She had to put away her fears of the ramifications she knew would follow for now.

His mouth came down on hers and she sighed into him, letting herself go. Savoring the defeat of her fears. Tasting his skin, she dug her fingers into his corded muscles. Soaking his strength into hers she gave freely and openly of hers. He lifted her hips and she wrapped her legs around his waist as she held his face against hers.

She gloried in his possession and saw his tensed jaw as he held back the demon. For a second she tensed, scared, then she gave up to the inevitable. She loved him. He was her soul mate. She had waited for him all her life. He thrust hard and she soared. Up, up and away. Then he withdrew and flipped her to her side. He cradled her from behind. Her buttocks cradled against his hardness.

Then she felt him nudge against her opening. Felt his tip entering her while he kissed along her collarbone. He licked and sucked at the pulse beating on the side of her neck. She welcomed him eagerly once again in her body. The rhythm of their need pounding in her heart until both were lost in the sensations once again.

Leo shuddered as the climax hit him. His fangs had descended, but he kept his face hidden in Eve's hair. He didn't want to frighten her, he but knew that while he could keep the demon leashed, he wouldn't be able to control some aspect of his personality in the throes of passion.

He needed her. Loved her. Cradling her, he fell asleep.

When they awoke, she shifted against him. "I must go." Her heart wrenched as he stroked her face tenderly.

"Stay." He whispered.

She must tell him now.

"Leo, we can't be together," she blurted out as she got up and started pulling her clothes back on.

"Why?" Leo sat up. His muscular chest distracted her. She looked her fill, memorizing every plane and angle of his body. Then she averted her eyes.

"My Gran…wouldn't let me be with you." She told him. "And I can't do this without her blessing."

"I love you and want to marry you." He said. She still didn't quite look at him and that bothered him. He missed her warmth. She was standing right there in front of him, but he could feel the walls going up around her. Like she was sealing herself off. "Are you scared of me?"

"No…I just proved that I'm not." She replied. "I feel you here—" she pointed to her chest, "—in my heart. I know you wouldn't hurt me, ever."

"Then let's get married."

"No. I can't. Not without my Gran's acceptance. I'm sorry, but there's no chance for that."

***

If he listened to her, he would leave her alone and let her go. She clearly wanted to go. Seeing her again, being with her again stirred up long buried desires and needs. Chest aching with regret, he couldn't avoid the gut wrenching loss. Was there any way he could get her to listen to him? Should he even try? Leo knew nothing good came the easy way. And Eve was the best thing to happen to him. He silently vowed not to give up.

He got up and started pulling on his clothes. "Let's go then."

"Where?"

"To see your Gran." He repeated. "Let's go."

"Why…what…what are you doing?" She asked him as he took her hand and started walking down the stairs.

"Do you love me?" Leo asked.

"Yes…yes. I do." She replied.

"Then no one can stand in our way. I won't let you go without a fight." Leo growled.

Shivering with anticipation, but happy at Leo for taking such a decisive way to fight for her, Eve followed him.

Oh, how she loved him.

Reaching her Gran's house, Eve walked in and invited Leo in.

"Come in. I'm sure Gran is here somewhere," she went in ahead. "I'll call her."

Gran put the knitting aside and looked up. "Where…" she started then halted when she saw Leo standing behind Eve.

Then Leo moved. He went on his knees in front of Eve's Gran. "Ms Hathaway, I'm here to ask for your granddaughter's hand in marriage." Smiling at her he asked very courteously.

Her grandmother looked flustered.

Eve's throat clogged with emotion. The wind blowing through the house brought goose bumps to her skin. She waited with bated breath for her Gran's answer.

Her grandmother wiped away at her eyes and nodded.

Looking towards Leo, she saw him watching her with that magnetic gaze. Eve smiled. And walked into his arms when he stood up.

<<<The End>>>

More Praise for **One Bite Leads to Another**

"One Bite Leads To Another is a very seductive read perfect for romance lovers, and it offers a wonderful gush of paranormal that'll satisfy the thirst for all who crave paranormal-romances.

Just as Eve found herself drawn to Leo, I also found myself drawn to him from the beginning. And who wouldn't? He's sexy, dangerous, and knows how to pleasure a woman. I'd let him bite me as many times as he wanted!

The story line is also captivating. Kelly Steel weaves a delicious mystery around Eve that'll make you want to uncover all the pieces to know the answers Leo seeks. She also does an amazing job creating the suspense. Everything twines together at the end beautifully in a way that won't disappoint. I can't wait for the sequel!"

Reader on Goodreads

Coming Soon…

One Bite *for* The Unborn

Eve is pregnant and Leo is not too happy about it. Then there are people wanting Eve and her baby dead. Who are these people? Would Eve manage to convince Leo that she would do anything to keep her baby? And would Leo be able to save Eve and her baby?

Medical Romance by Kelly Steel

Unexpected Reunion

Dr Amber Whippy has a secret from her ex-husband, Dr Jake McAllister. They had a passionate relationship and a stormy marriage, but would Jake take kindly to Amber keeping this secret?

www.ingramcontent.com/pod-product-compliance
Lightning Source LLC
Chambersburg PA
CBHW060956120626
46557CB00003B/1185